MARVEL
CAPTAIN
MARVEL

WHAT
MAKES
A HERO

WRITTEN BY
Pamela Bobowicz

PAINTINGS BY
Eda Kaban

MARVEL

LOS ANGELES · NEW YORK

PRINTED IN THE UNITED STATES OF AMERICA
FIRST EDITION, MARCH 2019
10 9 8 7 6 5 4 3
ISBN 978-1-368-04807-1
FAC-034274-19232
LIBRARY OF CONGRESS CONTROL NUMBER: 2018962750
REINFORCED BINDING

FOR MY GREATEST HEROES:
KYLE, LYNN AND RYAN. —PB

TO ALL THE SUPER LADIES
OUT THERE! —EK

BEFORE I HAD POWERS, I was a pilot in the US Air Force. I've always loved to fly—the feeling of going higher, further, faster ... of wanting *more*.

I'VE LEARNED THAT EVERYONE HAS POWER. IT'S NOT INDESTRUCTIBILITY OR FLYING OR SUPER-SPEED—IT'S THAT FIRE IN YOUR SOUL THAT PUSHES YOU TO TOUCH THE SKY.

Stepping up for those who need hope—something or someone to believe in—leads you to the greatest heights, and there, we all soar higher, further, faster.

SHURI

When my brother became the black panther, I knew my job would get harder. I had to design the defenses that would protect my king and my country.

It would've been easy to be jealous that T'Challa was king because he was born first. But easy's boring.

SCIENCE IS ANYTHING BUT BORING—it's innovation, and it's a chance to learn from our mistakes. Saving the world is the same way: We accept the challenge, then rise to the occasion. In the lab, I imagine the impossible, then create a way to bring it to life.

I MAY BE THE DAUGHTER OF LEGENDS, but I had to forge my own path.

My mother was my hero. But after she disappeared, I lost my way. I needed to find my strength again.

IT'S HARD TO SHINE WHEN YOU'RE STANDING IN THE SHADOWS OF HEROES, BUT THERE'S NOTHING BETTER THAN GETTING A CHANCE TO SHOW WHAT YOU'RE WORTH AND TAKING IT.

Be patient and fierce. Heroes need to be saved, too, and when the day comes where your dreams and ambitions collide, you'll be the kind of legend you looked up to.

WOULDN'T CALL MYSELF A HERO. I simply survived everything that was thrown my way.

I was thrown Gamora's way most often. We're sisters . . . and competitors.

No matter who we're fighting, though, we fight for what we believe is right.

It's taken us years, and we've chased each other across galaxies, but we've learned that sometimes, WE'RE STRONGER TOGETHER.

Heroes have to make hard choices, same as sisters. But a sacrifice made for love is the most heroic thing we've ever done.

SCARLET WITCH

My POWERS HAVEN'T ALWAYS BEEN A GIFT. In fact, they put me in a lot of danger until I learned who I could trust.

USING MY POWERS BECAUSE I *CAN* AND USING THEM BECAUSE I *SHOULD* ARE VERY DIFFERENT. BUT UNDERSTANDING MY ROLE IN A TEAM OF HEROES SHOWED ME THAT WE ALL HAVE A GREATER POWER THAT COMES FROM WITHIN: COMPASSION.

That power, if we accept it, helps us care for one another and stand side by side as we face our greatest challenges.

I DIDN'T INTEND TO EXIST AMONG SUPER HEROES.

I only wanted to do my job.

Responsibility sounds pretty straightforward, but it's more than keeping a schedule or running a company or expanding a vision into a global enterprise. IT'S BEING ABLE TO ATTACK A PROBLEM FROM ANY ANGLE. IT'S KNOWING WHERE TO PUSH AND WHEN TO PULL. And when heroism meets responsibility, it's sending the people you care about out to save the world, not knowing if they'll return.

Knowing who you are and what you're capable of in your own skin is more powerful than any suit of armor—it's what makes the ordinary extraordinary.

WHEN I BECAME GENERAL OF THE DORA MILAJE, I was already the greatest warrior Wakanda had ever known, sworn to protect Wakanda's leader.

IT'S NOT EASY TO PLEDGE YOURSELF TO A CAUSE. DUTY IS LIKE ARMOR. IT'S HEAVY, AND IT'S NOT ALWAYS COMFORTABLE. IT'S A PROMISE TO YOURSELF TO DO WHAT'S RIGHT.

When your courage is tested, remain calm. Remember why you started. Then run as fast as you can toward the fight, knowing that no matter how it ends, you've stayed true to your cause and to yourself. Loyalty and bravery, combined, are greater than any super-power.

I'M THE LAST OF MY KIND, A LEGENDARY WARRIOR SWORN TO PROTECT THE THRONE OF ASGARD.

When I left my home, I hid behind shame, anger, and regret. I'd failed my people, my sisters, and I had nothing to believe in. I learned the hard way that anger can be a destructive force.

WHEN YOU LOSE YOUR WAY, DIG DEEP. Harness the anger, rein it in, and then use it to fuel the goodness in your heart's deepest desires. That's how legends are made. That's how warriors rise again, born of ashes and willing to fight for what they believe in.

PEGGY CARTER

I JOINED THE ARMY TO FIGHT HATRED and evil in a time of crisis. Along the way I became part of a legacy of heroes.

Every journey begins with a first step, and the confidence to take that step and face whatever is thrown your way is one of the greatest super-powers of all. IT'S IMPORTANT THAT WE SPEAK UP FOR OURSELVES, BUT EVEN MORE IMPORTANT THAT WE SPEAK UP FOR THOSE WHO CANNOT.

Standing up for what is right is hard. But hold firm. Bravery comes in its own time, and there's no army stronger than good people standing together, come what may.

SOMETIMES I STILL DON'T BELIEVE I'M ONE OF THE EARTH'S GREATEST HEROES.

When I became a spy, it was my job to play any role I was handed without blowing my cover.

IT'S HARD TO REMEMBER WHO YOU ARE WHEN YOU SPEND SO MUCH TIME TRYING TO BE SOMEONE ELSE. SOMETIMES YOU HAVE TO TRY ON A NUMBER OF DIFFERENT MASKS TO SEE WHICH ONE FITS.

But take hold of your anchor, pull your friends close, and peel back the disguise. The hero you've always been will be right there, ready and waiting.

'M THE QUEEN MOTHER OF WAKANDA. When my husband was king, I raised our children to believe in our country, its people, and its legacy.

I knew T'Challa would need guidance when he took the throne. It's difficult to watch my children serve the wider world and all its people, BUT MY DUTY IS TO STAND BESIDE THEM AS COUNSEL, SUPPORTER, AND FRIEND IN WHATEVER COMES THEIR WAY. Through their eyes, I can see a wise, brave, daring future. I'm here to help them to take the first step.

LONG BEFORE I JOINED THE GUARDIANS, I discovered that emotions can be stronger than even the most indestructible Super-Soldier, mech suit, or alien warrior.

I'VE LEARNED THE HARD WAY THAT KNOWING HOW YOU FEEL AND BEING ABLE TO EXPRESS THOSE FEELINGS IS A POWER ALL ITS OWN. It's being brave enough to open up your heart to let someone see what's inside, and being kind enough to look into their eyes to see their hopes and dreams.

Never be afraid to feel deeply. Harness the root of your soul and pull it up to the surface to declare who you are. Seeing and being seen is one of the greatest powers of all.

NAKIA

WAKANDA IS A PEACEFUL PLACE full of stunning advancements and a rich, proud culture.

But beyond Wakanda's borders, things are different. There's inequality and suffering—a world that needs our help, one willing Wakandan at a time. HIDING FROM THE WORLD MAY KEEP YOU SAFE, BUT SAFETY MEANS NOTHING IF IT'S NOT A RIGHT FOR EVERYONE.

Be brave enough to advocate for those who cannot, and dare to dream of equality for all. That is how one person can save the world.

I'M MARIA RAMBEAU.

I'm Monica.

I used to fly with Carol Danvers. She was our friend.

Someone we could always count on.

It's difficult to say good-bye to family and hope they'll be the same when they come back.

It's sad and lonely, missing a friend.

We keep moving forward.

We do what we have to do.

DON'T LOSE HOPE. The day will come when you meet again. We look to the stars for guidance, for comfort, for direction. We, too, can be the guiding light that shines bright enough to lead someone back home.

FOR THE HERO IN ALL OF US...